A TASTE OF FRANCE

Roz Denny

RSVP

RAINTREE
STECK-VAUGHN
P U B L I S H E R S

The Steck-Vaughn Company

Austin, Texas

Titles in this series

France

India

Italy

Japan

Cover *Vines in front of a picturesque château in southwest France. France has many wine-producing regions.*

Frontispiece *A baker's shop on the island of Corsica. The French eat fresh bread with every meal.*

UK version copyright © 1994 Wayland (Publishers) Ltd.

U.S. version copyright © 1994 Thomson Learning

This edition published by Raintree Steck-Vaughn Publishers, an imprint of Steck-Vaughn Company.

Library of Congress Cataloging-in-Publication Data
Denny, Roz.
A taste of France / Roz Denny.
p.   cm. —(Food around the world)
Includes bibliographical references and index.
ISBN 0-8172-4895-1
1. Cookery, French—Juvenile literature. 2. Food habits—France—Juvenile literature.
[1. Cookery, French. 2. Food habits—France. 3. France—Social life and customs.]
I. Title. II. Series.
TX719.D388   1994
641.5944—dc20   93-37198

Printed in Italy. Bound in the United States.

Contents

France today

The French are known for their style. This country house looks pretty with its blue shutters and flower pots.

France is the largest country in Europe and one of the most important members of the European Community. It has a population of over 56 million people.

The French are famous throughout the world for their good taste, their great sense of style, and, most of all, for their excellent food.

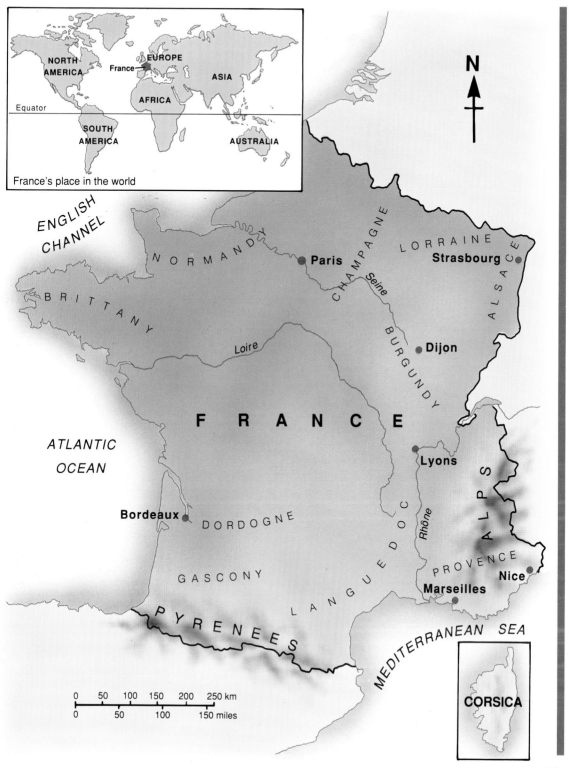

N

NORTH AMERICA
EUROPE
France
ASIA
AFRICA
Equator
SOUTH AMERICA
AUSTRALIA

France's place in the world

ENGLISH CHANNEL

NORMANDY

BRITTANY

Paris

CHAMPAGNE

LORRAINE

Strasbourg

ALSACE

Seine

Loire

BURGUNDY

Dijon

F R A N C E

ATLANTIC OCEAN

Lyons

ALPS

Bordeaux

DORDOGNE

LANGUEDOC

Rhône

PROVENCE

Nice

GASCONY

Marseilles

PYRENEES

MEDITERRANEAN SEA

| 0 | 50 | 100 | 150 | 200 | 250 km |

| 0 | 50 | 100 | 150 miles |

CORSICA

5

A taste of France

Most French people love good food. They expect to eat well at home, and they also expect delicious food when they eat out, whether in a simple street café, a bistro, or a fine restaurant. French children are brought up to think of food as an important part of life.

France once had colonies in Africa, North America, and the Far East. Many people from these former colonies have settled in France and have brought with them their own style of cooking. Today, dishes such as couscous (crushed wheat grain served with a meat or vegetable stew) from North Africa have become popular in France.

Many French dishes such as *boeuf bourguignon* and *quiche lorraine* have become popular outside France, and many of the words we use when discussing food and cooking are French. Some examples are chef, cuisine, restaurant, hors d'oeuvre, and omelette — and there are many others.

The regions

France has many different landscapes, from flat plains to mountains. There are plains in the central and northern parts of the country. The Alps are a mountain range that runs north from the

A farmhouse high up in the French Alps. In winter, tourists flock to the many ski resorts in the area.

A taste of France

The Loire River is surrounded by gently rolling countryside. This picture shows a vineyard, with open fields behind.

Mediterranean Sea, along the borders with Italy and Switzerland. The Pyrenees run along the border between France and Spain.

There is also a great difference in climate between the north and the south. In the south, where the land borders the Mediterranean Sea, the summers are hot and dry and the winters are mild. In the north, where the land borders the Atlantic Ocean and the English Channel, the winters are colder and the summers not as warm. And in the mountainous regions of the east, the summers are short and hot and the winters are long and cold.

Three important rivers wind their way through the countryside: the Seine, which flows through Paris; the Loire, which passes through some of the prettiest countryside in France; and the Rhône, which flows south to the Mediterranean.

Let's have a closer look at the different regions and their food.

Normandy and Brittany
Normandy and Brittany, in the northwest, are famous for their delicious food. Both Normandy and Brittany have historical links with Britain. King William I (known as William the Conqueror) was Duke of Normandy when he conquered England in 1066. Brittany is the land of an ancient race of

Normandy is famous for its soft cheese, unsalted butter, and Calvados (apple brandy).

people called Bretons. The Bretons were related to the ancient Britons of Wales and Cornwall in Britain. That is why the names Brittany and Britain are similar.

Normandy is flat with small fields and orchards enclosed by thick hedges. Cattle graze on the rich grass and produce milk for butter, cheese, and a thick, tart cream that the French call *crème fraîche*. The orchards produce juicy apples for desserts and for making into juice, cider, and an alcoholic drink called Calvados, which is a kind of apple brandy. Normandy's most famous cheese is Camembert, sold in round wooden boxes. When it is ripe, the center becomes very soft and creamy, almost runny, and begins to have a stronger smell.

Tarte aux pommes
This is a tart from Normandy. It is a crisp, sweet pastry filled with cream and a purée of apples, topped with more thinly sliced apples arranged in a pretty circle, then brushed with a shiny glaze of apricot jam.

A taste of France

Fishing is an important industry in the many harbor towns around the coast of Brittany.

Crêpes suzettes are orange-flavored, sweet pancakes.

Brittany has a lovely coastline with many small natural harbors, making it popular with fishermen and vacationers. Brittany is known for its fish, shellfish, and mollusks. Some mollusks, such as oysters, are often eaten raw by the French. Mussels (or *moules*) are a favorite food with fishermen, who eat them in a soup called *moules marinières.*

Brittany is also well known for its large thin pancakes, or crepes. Savory crepes are made of a grain called buckwheat (*blé noir* in French), which makes the pancakes look speckled with beige and black; sweet crepes are made with wheat flour. The batter is poured onto a large, round griddle stone and spread around very speedily with a kind of paddle. When cooked, crepes can be served with many different delicious fillings or toppings. It takes practice to become a good crepe maker.

The Loire valley

This beautiful valley is in the middle of France, on either side of France's longest river, the Loire. The pretty countryside has many vineyards, small farms, wooded valleys, and fruit orchards growing cherries, plums, apricots, pears, and apples. No wonder it is known as the "Garden of France." Many French kings and nobles of the past built fairy-tale castles, called châteaus, in the Loire valley.

The Loire valley is dotted with pretty, historic, riverside towns and villages.

A taste of France

The Champs Elysées in central Paris is a bustling street with many open-air cafés.

Paris

Paris is the capital city of France. It is not only the center of government for the country, it is famous world wide as a center of culture. Paris has a lot of wonderful shops, cafés, bistros, and fine restaurants. You often find farmers' markets in and around Paris selling vegetables, cheeses, fish, cold meats, herbs, spices, and special foods such as olives and dried fruits. The biggest and most famous market was called Les Halles, where the traders started work in the early hours of the morning while the rest of Paris slept. Then they would eat a delicious onion soup topped with bread and grated cheese for breakfast. The market at Les Halles was moved underground in 1979, and is now called Forum des Halles.

Soupe à l'oignon

French onion soup is made by frying onions, sliced into rings, until they are very brown and then cooking them in a rich, tasty stock. The soup is served with slices of French bread topped with toasted cheese.

Champagne

Champagne, the region to the west of Paris, gives its name to possibly the world's most famous white wine – champagne. This dry, sparkling wine is drunk at weddings and parties all over the world. The method of making champagne was developed by a churchman, Dom Perignon. The Champagne region is also the home of Brie cheese, which is very popular with children all over France. Brie is mild and creamy with a delicious rind, and looks like a Camembert cheese, only larger and flatter.

A vineyard in Champagne. The grapes are used to make the famous sparkling wine.

A taste of France

Strasbourg houses.
Both buildings and
food in Alsace are
very German in style.

Alsace

Alsace is a region next to Germany. Alsatians love to eat! The food and drink is German in style, with sausages, sauerkraut (a kind of sour, shredded cabbage), pork, goose, and game. The food is washed down with German-style lager or white wines with German names, such as Reisling. Strasbourg is the chief city of Alsace and home for the European Community Parliament.

Quiche lorraine

Lorraine is an area in northern France, near Alsace. It is famous for pastry, and especially for *quiche lorraine.* This is a savory custard filled with eggs, cream, and sliced onions. Sometimes grated cheese or pieces of chopped bacon (which the French call *lardons*) are also added.

Eating asparagus

A favorite vegetable in Strasbourg is white asparagus. In May, when it is freshly picked, you can see many people eating it in restaurants.

Asparagus is often eaten with the fingers: pick up a stalk at the cut end and take bites from the other end as neatly as possible.

Burgundy

Lovers of fine food and wine are called "gourmets" (pronounced *goor-mays*) by the French. Many gourmets think some of the best produce comes from Burgundy, which is in eastern France. Many of the world's top restaurants and finest chefs are in Burgundy. The big, industrial cities of Dijon and Lyons produce mustard, *foie gras* (rich and tender goose liver), sausages, and spicy gingerbreads called *pain d'épices*. Dishes described as "*à la dijonnaise*" have mustard in them, and "*à la lyonnaise*" have lots of onions and cream.

Boeuf bourguignon *is a rich beef stew.*

Burgundy stews

Burgundy is famous for stews and casseroles cooked using the local wine. *Boeuf bourguignon* is made from cubes of tender beef cooked slowly in red wine with onions, garlic, and *lardons*. A splash or two of brandy is added just before serving. *Coq au vin* (right) is another famous dish from Burgundy. It is a delicious, rich casserole of chicken cooked in red wine.

Sunflower seeds are made into cooking oil.

Bordeaux

Bordeaux in the southwest is a world-famous wine region. It is known mostly for red wine, which is also called claret (after the French word for clear, *clairet*). There are also fields of sunflowers and corn, which are used to make cooking oils. In the forests, free-range chickens are raised.

Nearby Gascony is known for hearty, country-style dishes using lamb, seafood, sausages, and beans.

The south of France

Here lie the regions of Provence and Languedoc, which are hot, dry, and sunny. The ground is stony and the soil thin. The crops that grow best in the south of France are olive trees (some of which are a great many years old); grapes that are made into wine; and fragrant herbs, such as rosemary, thyme, lavender, and bay. The big cities of Nice and Marseilles are important seaports, and the dishes served here include colorful fish soups (known as *bouillabaisse*) and sunny salads of tomatoes, beans, and olives.

Vineyards and olive groves are features of southern France.

Purple lavender is used in perfume.

Bouillabaisse

The best-known version of this delicious fish stew comes from Marseilles, on the south coast. Lots of different Mediterranean fish are cooked in fish stock with olive oil, herbs, and tomatoes. *Bouillabaisse* is served with chunks of French bread with *rouille* (a spicy egg and oil paste).

Nearby is the marshy area of the Camargue, where white horses are allowed to roam. In this unusual part of France, rice is grown and French "cowboys" tend small black cattle. These people are always on the move with their herds of animals. As a result, they have developed a tradition of barbecuing their meat over an open fire wherever they camp for the night.

Salade niçoise

This salad from Nice, in the south of France, is a main course in itself. It is usually made with cooked green beans and potatoes tossed with tomatoes, olives, onions, tuna fish, hard-boiled eggs, and anchovies (little salty fish).

The Dordogne

The Dordogne, which is inland from the Mediterranean, has cool, woody valleys. This area was very important in prehistoric times. Here, thousands of years ago, people hunted big animals such as mammoths, gathered berries, and fished. You can still see their vivid, bright cave paintings at Lascaux. Nowadays, the people still hunt for rare underground mushrooms, known as truffles, at the foot of oak trees. They raise geese for *foie gras*, grow walnuts, and produce honey.

A prehistoric cave painting at Lascaux.

Geese are raised for their livers.

Farming in France

France is a rich agricultural country that produces a great variety of foods, including many delicacies that are exported all over the world. Generally speaking, French farmers have quite small farms, and they take great pride in what they grow. Often they form groups, called cooperatives, to help each other out when it comes to harvesting and selling their goods.

Most French farms are small and family-run.

A farmer with a cart and oxen. Old-fashioned farming methods like this are now rare.

Cheeses
There are over 300 different cheeses made in France from three types of milk – cows', goats', and sheep's milk.

Many cheeses, such as Brie, are now popular around the world, while others are local specialties from small cheese makers, maybe even from one farm.

Next time you look at a grocery store or supermarket cheese display, look at the French cheeses and see how different they are in shape, size, and color. There are hard cheeses such as Cantal; cheeses with soft rinds and creamy insides such as Brie and Camembert; small, tangy goats'-milk cheeses, called *chèvres*; and blue cheeses such as Roquefort with thin green-blue lines through them.

French cheeses come in all shapes, sizes, and types – hard and soft, large and small. They can be found in grocery stores all over the world.

Garlic is an essential ingredient in French cooking. The bulbs of garlic are hung on strings for storing.

Vegetables and Fruits

With such a good climate and fertile soils it is not surprising that France grows so many wonderful fruits and vegetables. Onions, shallots (small purple onions), and garlic give a spicy, savory flavor to stews, soups, and salads. Cauliflower, asparagus, eggplant, peppers (red, green, and yellow), carrots, celery, endive, zucchini, fennel, globe artichokes, tomatoes, turnips, and spinach are popular vegetables in France and are grown in many areas. The French like a variety of fruits including apples of all sizes and colors, apricots, cherries, black currants, kiwis, peaches, pears, plums (many of which are dried to make prunes), and lovely fresh nuts such as almonds, walnuts, and hazelnuts.

The French enjoy gathering wild mushrooms and truffles from fields and woodlands. Sometimes a pet pig or dog is trained to snuffle out underground truffles, and then the owner must try to get them before the animal gobbles them up. Older children learn what to look for. Any newly discovered truffle sites are kept a closely guarded secret – truffles can fetch very high prices at market.

A truffle is a kind of underground mushroom. Truffles are great delicacies and are very expensive.

Melons, plums, apricots, and peaches are popular summer fruits.

The history of French cuisine

Marie de Médicis. This Italian princess brought a love of good cooking to France.

In 1600, an Italian princess, Marie de Médicis, traveled to France to marry the dashing new French king, Henri IV, who had won the throne after many years of fighting. Marie brought fine Italian cooks to France.

With such delicious food being served, Henri's new court of nobles and their ladies decided eating well was an extremely pleasurable pastime. They began to copy the Italian cooks. *Haute cuisine*, or "high cooking," became fashionable, and elegant ladies of the court enjoyed pretending to be cooks or milkmaids churning butter.

The peasants, though, had to wait until the French Revolution of 1789 in order to enjoy fine food. By 1792 the king, Louis XVI, had been overthrown by the French people. The king and many nobles lost their heads under the guillotine, so their chefs lost their jobs.

This picture, La cuisinière (the cook), dates from 1753. Her fine dress shows that she was probably a fashionable woman playing "cook."

A taste of France

Fashionable women at a Paris cake shop in 1889.

As a result, many of these chefs moved to the big cities and started selling fine foods to the ordinary townspeople in inns and food stores. These became known as restaurants.

Chefs gradually became more popular and important in France. Famous chefs, such as Antonin Carême and Alexis Soyer, were admired all over Europe. Today, French chefs such as Paul Bocuse and Roger Vergé still hold great influence in the world of cooking. Cooking in any great restaurant kitchen is like conducting a well-organized army with the chef (or chief) at the head. Well-trained staff know exactly what to do to produce delicious meals within minutes of an order.

Chefs at work in a restaurant kitchen.

Shopping for food in France

The French believe it is not only important to cook well, but just as important to shop well. In fact, it is possible to buy such good food in France that you may not even have to do any cooking. Even the smallest village has its own bakery, called a *boulangerie*, where the baker gets up in the very early hours of the morning, about 3 a.m., to bake fresh, crusty bread. The French buy fresh bread at least twice a day, normally the long, thin bread sticks called baguettes, which they carry home under their arms. You can also buy croissants and cakes at a *boulangerie.*

Fresh meat is sold in butchers' shops, or *boucheries.* French cooks expect well-cut meat and are very particular about what they buy. They also use less popular parts of the animal, such as the trotters (pigs' feet), head, and ears, which can be cooked slowly in delicious ways.

Cold, cooked meats and pork are sold in shops called *charcuteries.* The *charcutier*, or pork butcher, often makes his own pâtés (called *rillettes*) and

People carrying fresh bread from the bakery are a familiar sight on French streets.

27

A taste of France

Above *Markets sell fresh farm produce.* Below *Supermarkets have counters for different foods.*

sausages, and offers a tempting display of sliced salami.

There are bustling markets held in most towns and cities where local farmers take their fresh produce to sell – butter, cheese, eggs, farm chickens, and homegrown vegetables, as well as special local foods such as walnuts, honey, olives, and herbs.

Even big modern French supermarkets divide their stores into smaller units to look like mini-shops under the same roof. There will be a *charcuterie* counter, a *boulangerie*, a *poissonnerie* for fish, and a *pâtisserie* for small fancy cakes and pastries.

What French children like to eat

French children are brought up to eat the same foods as the rest of the family. Children often eat out with their parents in bistros, and even fine restaurants, which are happy to serve children the same food as their parents but in half-size portions. French children tend to eat snacks less often than children in other Western countries, but they still enjoy burgers; French fries (which they call *frites*); toasted cheese and ham sandwiches, called *croque-monsieur*; and apple tarts, or *tarte aux pommes.*

Children and adults gather together for a family Sunday lunch.

29

A taste of France

Croissants, dipped in frothy, milky coffee, are usually eaten only as a weekend treat, often on Sunday morning.

Breakfast in France might be a cup of hot, steaming, milky chocolate with chunks of crusty baguette and apricot *confiture* (jam), or chocolate and hazelnut spread. Packaged cereals such as cornflakes are popular too, but croissants are eaten on weekends.

School lunches are tasty and popular with children. There is always a salad starter, such as grated carrot or radish, followed by meat or fish and vegetables. After this there is cheese, fruit, yogurt, and *petits-suisses* (little pots of creamy, fresh white cheese), and maybe even a slice of cake, especially if there is a festival to celebrate.

At home the main meal, which is often in the evening, might be a delicious light stew called a *pot-au-feu* in which meat and vegetables are cooked slowly in a stock, or bouillon.

A *pot-au-feu* is often divided into separate courses: the *bouillon* is served first ladled into bowls as a soup, then the meat and vegetables are served afterward. It is acceptable to use the same knife and fork throughout the meal, resting them on small bars on the table in between courses. Chunks of crusty bread are used to mop up delicious juices and sauce; butter is not served (except with soft cheeses). Cheese is eaten next, followed by fresh fruit and maybe a delicious sweet pastry or two. A lighter evening meal is called *souper* in French and may be just a bowl of soup with more bread, cheese, and fruit.

Pot-au-feu *is a dish of boiled meat and vegetables.*

Le pique-nique

The Picnic, *by Claude Monet, painted in 1866. Monet was one of France's greatest painters.*

The French enjoy eating outdoors. Picnic areas can be found throughout the countryside.

French food is ideal to pack for a picnic. Why not plan a picnic in the style of some of the great French painters, such as Renoir or Monet?

Plan a shopping trip as you would if you were in France, visiting first the baker to buy a long, crusty loaf of French bread, or baguette. Then visit a cheese and cold meat counter in a delicatessen to choose two cheeses (one hard and one soft), and two sliced cold meats, or a pâté and one cold meat. Allow about 2 ounces of cheese and pâté and 1 ounce of meat for each person. (The French use very little meat on a sandwich.) Buy some crisp apples, ripe tomatoes, a bottle of mineral water, and fruit juice. Then perhaps treat yourself to a cake or pastry. Take along a cutting board or plate for the meats and cheese, plus table knives for spreading. Pack everything in a large basket and cover with a checked tablecloth to spread on the ground.

Put together your own pique-nique with bread, cheese, cold meat, fruit, and mineral water.

Vinaigrette

Ingredients

6 tablespoons olive or
  vegetable oil
2 tablespoons wine or
  cider vinegar
½ teaspoon salt
about 4 good
  grindings of black
  pepper
1 teaspoon French
  mustard, such as
  Dijon
1 teaspoon clear
  honey

Equipment

screw-top jar with lid
pepper mill
measuring spoons

Make vinaigrette in a screw-top jar and store it in the refrigerator.

Simply spoon everything into the jar, screw on the lid firmly, and shake well. It will instantly blend together. If you let vinaigrette stand for a few minutes, you will notice the oil and vinegar separating. Just give it another shake before serving.

Salade mesclun

You can serve vinaigrette with a simple mixed salad of lettuce leaves, which the French call *salade mesclun*. Either buy a bag of mixed salad leaves from the supermarket, or two or three whole lettuces of different kinds.

1 Wash the chosen leaves well and pat dry with paper towel.

2 Tear into pieces and place in a salad bowl.

3 Trickle over about half the vinaigrette and mix well with your hands, which should be very clean! Eat as soon as possible.

Ingredients

Choose from the following:
Boston lettuce
escarole, or *frisée* (which is French for frizzy)
radicchio (small red lettuce)
Bibb lettuce
red-tip lettuce
watercress or argula
young dandelion leaves from the garden (called *pissenlit* in French)

Equipment

colander
salad spinner (if you have one)
paper towel
a big salad bowl

Omelette aux fines herbes

Ingredients

Serves 1–2

2 eggs
small handful of fresh
   parsley
a few stalks of fresh
   chives
a little sprig of thyme
   or few sprigs of
   chervil
1 tablespoon of butter
2 teaspoons of oil
salt
ground black pepper

Equipment

bowl
whisk or fork
small cup or pitcher
kitchen scissors
spatula
medium-sized, non-
   stick frying pan
warm plate

1   Break the eggs into a bowl, then beat well with the whisk or fork, adding a little salt and pepper.

2 Snip the herbs into little pieces with the scissors, into the cup.

3 Heat the butter and oil in the frying pan until it stops foaming; swirl it around the pan.

Always be careful when frying. Ask an adult to help you.

4 Pour in the eggs. Using a spatula and holding the pan handle with the other hand, pull back the sides of the omelette as it begins to set and let the runny egg slip underneath.

5 Continue like this until it is all lightly set, then sprinkle in the herbs.

6 Tip the pan away from you and flip one half of the omelette on top of the other, then slide it onto a warm plate. Serve hot.

Cassoulet

This is a quick-cooking version of a traditional French favorite (below).

Ingredients
Serves 3–4

1 small onion, peeled
2 strips lean bacon
1 tablespoon olive or
   vegetable oil
1 clove garlic, peeled
15 oz. can chopped or
   crushed tomatoes
15 oz. can white
   kidney beans
$\frac{2}{3}$ cup water
2 thick pork sausages,
   cooked, or 4–5 oz.
   smoked pork
   sausage
3–4 tablespoons dried
   breadcrumbs
salt
ground black pepper

Always be careful when frying, boiling, and grilling. Ask an adult to help you.

Equipment

chopping board and
knife
garlic press
can opener
strainer
medium saucepan
wooden stirrer
ovenproof dish
oven mitts

3 Bring to a boil, then turn down to a gentle simmer for 20 minutes, stirring occasionally. Meanwhile, cut the cooked sausages into thick chunks.

1 Cut the onion in half then into thin slices. Chop the bacon and place both in a medium saucepan with the oil. Crush in the garlic. Fry gently for 5 minutes, stirring.

4 Add the sausage to the pot and cook for a further 5 minutes. Pour into a shallow ovenproof dish and top with the breadcrumbs.

2 Open the cans of tomatoes and beans, and drain the beans through a strainer. Stir the tomatoes and beans into the pan and add the water.

5 Put under a preheated broiler and lightly brown the crumbs. Cool slightly before serving or you might burn your mouth.

Croque-monsieur

French toasted cheese and ham sandwiches are very popular with children. The one pictured below is an open sandwich made using a baguette.

Ingredients
Serves 4

¼ lb Gruyère cheese
1 egg
1 tablespoon milk
8 slices bread
butter, softened for
  spreading
4 slices lean ham

Equipment

table knife
bread board
bowl
whisk or fork
grater
cookie sheet
spatula
spoon
oven mitts

1 Preheat the broiler by turning it to the highest setting. If you use a toaster-oven, remove the broiler pan first.

Always be careful when using a hot broiler. Ask an adult to help you.

2 Grate the cheese on the biggest holes of the grater. Beat the egg and milk together then stir in the cheese.

3 Toast one side of the bread slices under the broiler – but only very lightly. Remove from the heat and spread a thin layer of butter on the untoasted side of each slice.

4 Put ham on the buttered side of four slices and top with the rest, pressing down well.

5 Spoon the eggy cheese mixture on top of each sandwich as neatly as you can, spreading it to the edges.

6 Place sandwiches on a cookie sheet (or toaster-oven pan) until the cheese melts and bubbles. Remove carefully using oven mitts and lift each sandwich onto plates with a spatula. Eat with your fingers or a knife and fork.

Ratatouille

A lovely vegetable stew from the south of France. It can be eaten hot or cold.

Equipment

kitchen knife for
  chopping
chopping board
garlic press
heavy-based saucepan
  with a lid
wooden spoon
can opener
serving dish

Ingredients

Serves 4

1 onion, peeled
1 clove garlic,
  peeled
1 green pepper,
  cut in half
1 small eggplant
2 zucchini

3 tablespoons olive oil
15 oz. can chopped or
  crushed tomatoes
1 teaspoon dried
  mixed herbs (such
  as thyme, oregano,
  or parsley)
salt
ground black pepper

1 Cut the onion in half then chop it in chunks. Put into the saucepan. Crush the garlic into the pan.

2 Cut out the core and stalk from the pepper and slice the flesh. Add this to the pan.

3 Chop the stalks off the eggplant and zucchini and cut the flesh into thick slices. Put to one side.

4 Add 2 tablespoons of oil to the pan with the onions and heat slowly until the vegetables start to cook.

5 Fry gently or *"sauté"* (the French word for this) for 5 minutes, stirring the pan once or twice.

6 Add another tablespoon of oil, together with the eggplant and zucchini. Stir well and cover the pan. Cook gently for 5 minutes, stir, then cook again for another 5 minutes.

7 Stir in the tomatoes and add the herbs, salt, and pepper to taste. Bring to a boil, then cover and cook gently for 15 minutes. Let it cool, then pour into a serving bowl.

French hot chocolate

This is a treat for weekend breakfasts. Use the best cooking chocolate you can for a good chocolaty taste. It is best to have an adult to help you at the stove.

Ingredients
Serves 1–2

2 oz. unsweetened or
  semi-sweet baking
  chocolate
1¼ cups whole creamy
  milk
1–2 teaspoons sugar
cocoa powder

Equipment

saucepan
wooden spoon
large cup and saucer

1　Break the chocolate up
into pieces and put it in the
saucepan with the milk.

Always be careful with
hot liquid. Ask an adult
to help you.

2　Heat slowly on the stove,
stirring occasionally with the
spoon until smooth. Add
sugar to taste.

3　Bring carefully to a boil so
that the milk becomes a little
frothy, then remove (carefully
again) from the stove and pour
into a cup or mug.

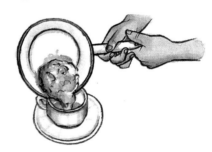

4　Sprinkle cocoa powder on
top and then drink when it
has cooled down a little.

Glossary

Bistro A simple restaurant that serves simple food, coffee, rolls, wine, and juices.

Chef A head cook in a restaurant or hotel. "Chef" means "chief" in French.

Colony A land that is governed by another country.

Cuisine The French word for kitchen. Nowadays, cuisine also means a style or type of cooking from any country.

Delicacy A type of food that is considered very special and delicious.

European Community A group of countries in Europe that have joined together to help each other with trade, agriculture, and finance.

Fertile When referring to soil, fertile means very rich and nourishing, thus encouraging plants to grow.

Free-range Animals raised for food, but permitted to roam freely instead of being caged.

Game Wild animals hunted for food and sport.

Gourmet A person who is a good judge of food and drink.

Graze To feed on grass.

Griddle A large, flat, heavy, metal plate or pan for cooking.

Guillotine An instrument for beheading people with a heavy blade that is dropped from above.

Herbs Shrubby plants that smell delicious and give a good flavor when used in cooking.

Hors d'oeuvres Small pieces of food served before a meal.

Lager A light beer brewed slowly and fermented at a low temperature.

Mammoth An extinct type of hairy elephant with long tusks that curved up. Mammoths once lived in Europe, Asia, and North America, but died out many thousands of years ago.

Mollusk An animal such as a clam, oyster, or mussel with a soft body enclosed in a shell of one or more sections.

Savory Having a good salty or spicy flavor; not sweet.

Seafood Fish and shellfish from the sea.

Stock The liquid produced when meat, bones, or vegetables are simmered in water and herbs.

Vineyards Fields where grapes are grown. The plants are called vines.

Further information

Information books:

France in Pictures.
Minneapolis: Lerner
Pulications, 1991.

Harris, Jonathan. *The Land
and People of France.* New
York: HarperCollins
Children's Books, 1989.

James, Ian. *France.* Inside.
New York: Franklin Watts,
1989.

Milner, Cate. *France.* World in
View. Austin: Raintree
Steck-Vaughn, 1990.

Moss, Peter and Palmer,
Thelma. *France.*
Enchantment of the World.
Chicago: Children's Press,
1986.

Recipe books:

Loewen, N. *Food in France.*
Vero Beach, FL: Rourke
Publications, 1991.

Waldee, Lynne M. *Cooking the
French Way.* Minneapolis:
Lerner Publications, 1982.

Wilkes, Angela. *My First
Cookbook.* New York: Alfred
A. Knopf, 1989.

Picture acknowledgments
The publishers would like to thank the following for allowing their photographs to be reproduced: Anthony Blake Photo Library 10 bottom, 14 bottom, 15, 16 top, 18, 21, 34, 36, 42; Bridgeman Art Library 24 (Prado, Madrid), 26 top (Giraudon), 32 top (Pushkin Museum, Moscow); Michael Busselle's Photolibrary *cover*; Cephas 16 bottom (M. Rock), 17 top (M. Rock), 26 bottom (M. Rock), 32 bottom (S. Boreham); E.T. Archive 25; Greg Evans Photo Library *frontispiece* (M. Wells), 12 (G.B. Evans), 20 top, (R. Van Raders), 30 (G.B. Evans); Eye Ubiquitous 33, 44; Denis Hughes-Gilbey 19 bottom, 26 bottom, 31, 38, 40; Tony Stone Worldwide 4 (M. Busselle), 8 (C. Waite), 9 (S. and N. Geary), 10 top (P. Cade), 11 (S. Studd), 14 top (C. Waite), 17 bottom (M. Busselle), 22, 28 top; Topham 7, 19 top, 23 both, 27; Wayland Picture Library *cover inset* (A. Blackburn), 6 (C. Fairclough), 20 bottom (C. Fairclough), 29 (C. Fairclough); Zefa 13 (Streichan).

The artwork on page 5 was supplied by Peter Bull. The recipe artwork on pages 34-45 was supplied by Judy Stevens.

Index